The Misadventures of SWEETIE PIE

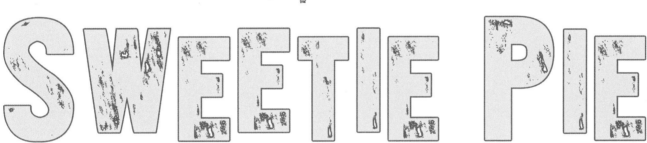

In memory of Marmalade and Little Gray

This paperback edition first published in 2018 by Andersen Press Ltd.
First published in Great Britain in 2015 by Andersen Press Ltd.,
20 Vauxhall Bridge Road, London SW1V 2SA.
Published by special arrangement with Houghton Mifflin Harcourt Publishing Company,
and Rights People, London.

Printed and bound in Malaysia.

1   3   5   7   9   10   8   6   4   2

British Library Cataloguing in Publication Data available.

ISBN 978 1 78344 292 8

The Misadventures of
SWEETIE PIE

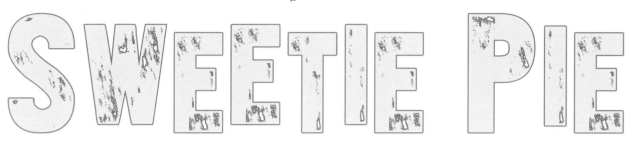

CHRIS VAN ALLSBURG

ANDERSEN PRESS

"He's sooo sweet!" squealed the pigtailed girl. The hamster had heard these words before. He'd once shared his home with a dozen friends. One by one, they'd all been taken away.

He'd been left behind because whenever a child had picked him up, he'd squirmed and scratched.

Today he did not put up a fight. Wherever his friends had gone, he wanted to go there too.

He left the pet shop and saw, for the first time, the great outdoors. It was filled with sunlight and endless blue sky, with smells he'd never smelled and wind he'd never felt.

In his new home Pigtails held him constantly, asking over and over, "Aren't you my little Sweetie Pie?" Since it was the only time he was let out of his small cage, he pretended to like it.

One afternoon Sweetie Pie awoke to find that his cage had been moved. Something else rested in its place. Pigtails sat in front of it for hours at a time.

The girl didn't ignore him completely, though. Each morning she dropped extra-large handfuls of food into his bowl.

Because it was so tasty, and because he had nothing else to do, he ate every bite.

Many days passed this way, until Pigtails brought a friend to meet Sweetie Pie. "Kind of big, isn't he?" the boy asked, holding an animal that felt more like a water balloon.

"Yeah," agreed Pigtails, "he eats too much, but he's lots of fun to play with. Is it a deal?" The boy handed over a few wrinkled notes and picked up the cage.

For the second time in his life, the hamster felt the wind in his fur and smelled the great outdoors. He breathed in deeply, but was back inside before he exhaled.

The boy put the cage
beside his bed and left the room.
Sweetie Pie heard a loud sniffing
sound.

The cage began to shake,
then crashed to the floor.
Sweetie Pie, his peanut-sized
heart pounding wildly, dug
out from under the wood chips
and found himself facing a
snarling dog.

"No, Buster!" The boy ran
back in the room. "He just wants
to be friends," he explained to
Sweetie Pie, pulling the dog
away.

Over the next few weeks,
Buster came into the room again
and again, knocking the cage to
the floor and banging his wet
black nose against the wire bars.

Sweetie Pie was too nervous to eat, and had bad dreams about mad dogs. He awoke from one of them when he felt his cage tilting again.

This time it was the boy carrying him to the front door. A car stopped in front of the house. A young girl jumped out and ran up the steps. "Can I hold him, can I hold him, can I hold him?" she asked. Cousin Sue clutched the hamster as if he were a fistful of sweets. Then she carried him away.

At home, Cousin Sue couldn't wait to play with her new pet.

She grabbed Sweetie Pie and yanked his bony paws through the sleeves of a pink dress. "Aren't you pretty?" Sue asked, then dropped him into the doll's house. He spun like a top, making a terrible mess. "That's not polite," she said, and tossed him back into his cage.

Sweetie Pie spent the day chewing his way out of the dress. He'd just finished when Cousin Sue returned. "Look, I got a present for you." She twisted a plastic ball open, stuck Sweetie Pie inside, and ran outdoors.

When Sue put the ball on the pavement, the nervous hamster clawed wildly. He shot along the pavement, picking up speed as he raced downhill.

The ball landed in a pile of leaves. Exhausted, Sweetie Pie waited for the girl to rescue him, but she never came.

The sun set and the moon rose. The lonely hamster spent the night staring at the stars, wondering if he'd ever get out of his plastic prison.

In the morning he saw children playing nearby. He pawed frantically and threw himself against the ball. Slowly, it began to tilt, then rolled off the pile of leaves. Sweetie Pie steered himself toward the children.

When the ball came to a stop at her feet, a little girl picked it up.

"Look," she said. "It's a hamster! I always wanted one of these, but my mum says no." She gazed at the hamster longingly. "I'm keeping him."

At home, she snuck Sweetie Pie into her room, opened the ball, and put him in a shoebox. When her mother called, she left.

Sweetie Pie's nose began to twitch. The hungry hamster smelled food. He climbed out of the box and followed the scent to the kitchen, where the girl sat eating. As he crossed the room, he heard a loud shriek. Then, BAM! Something hit the kitchen floor behind him, and a rush of air sent Sweetie Pie tumbling under the table.

"A rat!" the girl's mother yelled, raising her broom for another blow. The girl dropped to the floor to rescue Sweetie Pie and begged to keep him. "Not in this house," her mother answered.

The next day, the girl took Sweetie Pie to school, where he became the class pet. Each morning a different group of children would feed him and play with him, but when lessons began, he went back into his cage. He spent the rest of the day watching the leaves fall and the squirrels running through the trees.

Occasionally, one of the bushy-tailed animals came and sat on the windowsill.

The squirrel watched closely as the children opened and closed the cage. The hamster wondered if the squirrel was laughing at him – a silly little animal turned into a plaything for children.

When the Christmas holidays began, Sweetie Pie left with a boy who'd asked to take care of him. On his way home, the boy stopped at the playground with his friends.

The hamster wondered how long the boys would play. He curled into a ball. He loved being outdoors but was not used to the cold. When he finally looked around, Sweetie Pie saw the boys had left and that something strange was falling from the sky.

Before long, a blanket of white covered the wood chips in his cage. The sky got darker and the air grew colder. His teeth rattled, and Sweetie Pie suddenly felt bone-tired. He wished he could stop shaking.

Soon, his wish was granted. The hamster became still. His eyes closed and he fell into a deep and frigid sleep.

After the holidays the children came back to school and saw the empty cage. The boy who'd left Sweetie Pie at the playground described, with tears rolling down his cheeks, how he'd run back through the snow the next morning. He found the cage with its door open, and no sign of the hamster.

The teacher explained that someone must have rescued him. "I'm sure," she said, "a nice little boy or girl is taking care of him." The children knew better. Their forgetful classmate probably left the cage unlatched. The hamster had escaped and was now buried under a snowdrift, frozen stiff as an ice lolly.

This made them very sad, but not for long. The next week, a guinea pig one of the children received for Christmas moved in to Sweetie Pie's old cage.

By the time spring arrived, all the children, except for one, had forgotten about Sweetie Pie. The boy who'd left him outside could not stop worrying that, with the snow melted, the hamster's body would be discovered.

During break time, he could not keep his eyes from searching beneath bushes and dried leaves. Where could Sweetie Pie be?

If the boy had looked up instead of down, he would have found the answer. High above the playground, a pair of squirrels moved quickly through the trees.

They crawled into a leaf-filled hollow, made warm by their friends who were nesting there. The squirrels cracked off pieces of acorn with their sharp teeth and shared the food with their small, tailless comrade.

It was not as tasty as the food
he'd had when he was younger,
but looking out of the nest, with
his friends right behind him and
the children thirty feet below,
with no bars between him and the
deep blue sky, Sweetie Pie felt like
the luckiest squirrel in the tree.